PHINEIAD

A BRIEF HISTORY OF THE FUTURE

E.L. BROOKS

CONTENTS

ACKNOWLEDGEMENTS

I offer my gratitude to the friends, in person or online, who have offered comment and criticism in the final stages of editing this poem.

Thank you also to the angelic forces that have preserved my mind from the madness that has so often been the fall of poets.

Lastly, a particular thanks to my all-beautiful, ever-faithful wife, whose very presence is a balm, healing all wounds of worry and anxiety, for designing the cover and interior of this book, and grudgingly allowing these words to be printed.

PREFACE

There is no need for another defense of poetry. Attempts to explain the value of verse have already been made by those who view it as a force of tradition, and by those who see it as a force of progress; by atheistic voices who want it to charm a flattened world, and religious voices who believe poetry is necessary to break the materialist limitations of mundane speech. Much has been said that is true, that is worth hearing, and has convinced those who are willing to be convinced.

The reality is more fundamental than any argument can suggest. It is only a matter of having one's head on straight, of seeing the value of civilization or of being blind to it. Poetry has been with us since our earliest history. It is one of the few human things providing continuity between that dim and fragmentary time and our own. An age that sees no value in marriage, in property, in sacrifice, in praise, in any other constant of human life, also will not see the value of poetry, and no true argument for it seems possible unless we are already within that stream of civilization.

My own connection to the art cannot be reasonably accounted for. As a child, I loved books on natural science, often preferring them over stories, imagining that I would grow up to be a physicist or an engineer. I enjoyed some children's poetry but did not particularly identify with it. In 4th grade I found my mother's book of Emily Dickinson. Though I understood very little, it planted in me the belief that there was something more profound in it that I would like to be capable of knowing. Throughout adolescence this sense grew until reading and writing poetry became central to my identity. In my late teens I read the Kalevala and Paradise Lost and was given a further sense that I did not want to write just any poetry, but must eventually turn my attention to the composition of a Great Work. I cannot explain why this thought came to me with a sense of duty, nor can I avoid it.

Today there is much going by the name of poetry that would not be recognizable as such even one hundred years ago. There is also a steady revival of traditional verse. It generally seems to me that this revival wants to pick up where Robert Frost left off, to write works that are common, accessible, and profoundly human. There is little will to match or exceed the great works of the past. The book before you is not such a work, but is a preview of what ambitious poems I hope may be possible in the future.

The Phineiad is a book that looks to the past and future simultaneously. Looking backwards, it draws from medieval Romance and Allegory, the true genres of Christendom. Romance, at least in its most idealistic mode, transforms the violence of classical epic through Christian virtue, aimed at the defense of the innocent and powerless rather than of the tribe. It envisions a world in which love for a woman might civilize a man and encourage him to great works, rather than turning him to jealousy and conflict. Allegory envisions a hierarchical cosmology in which the mundane events and figures of our experience reflect a hidden, divine order. These are not genres that happened to be popular in the Christian age but are inextricably tied to it. But many conservative literary works are filled with a sense of loss, of longing for an order that has been shattered beyond repair, while the Phineiad is a story of restoration pointing toward the future.

It is an ambitious work in the large number of things that it attempts in a short space. It is at once a popularly written fairytale, and a poem full of abstract philosophical reflection; it is full of allusions to the Bible and to medieval literature, but understandable without knowledge of any of it; it places absurd humor side by side with difficult, serious reflections. It is by no means a perfect book, and not likely to be a popular one, but it is something of a microcosm of what I hope someday may be done on a grand scale.

E. L. B.

Chicago, Spring 2020

And behold one of the children of Israel went in before his brethren to a harlot of Madian, in the sight of Moses, and of all the children of Israel, who were weeping before the door of the tabernacle. And when Phinees the son of Eleazar the son of Aaron the priest saw it, he rose up from the midst; of the multitude, and taking a dagger, went in after the Israelite into the brothel house, and thrust both of them through together, to wit, the man and the woman in the genital parts. And the scourge ceased from the children of Israel.

Numbers 25

"Is this Jhesus the juster," quod I, "that Juwes did to deth,
Or is it Pierres the Plowman? Who paynted hym so rede?"

Langland

I

1. When baby Fin woke up that day
   He knew that he was brave.
   > No more would he weep at the dark,
   > Or need protection in the park.
   > He heard a voice within say, "hark,
   This life is yours to lose or save."

2. Fin boldly walked to the front door
   Making no pretence to hide.
   > He looked his mother in the eye,
   > Said, "on the winds of fortune I now fly.
   > To live without glory is to die.
   Comfort and ease are beneath my pride."

3. His mother wept, "My Fin! My Fin!
   Yesterday you supped at my breast.
   > Your legs have barely learned to walk,
   > Your lips barely begun to talk,
   > You cry when you scrape upon the rock.
   I protect you as my child, not house you as my guest."

4. "O mother dear, I'm man enough.
    It's only a moment to decide.
        I see grown men who never dare
        To leap out from their mother's care,
        To seek a life noble and fair.
    They replace her with the state, a job, or with a bride.

5. "But Virtue's strength ennobles us
    Who by providence are born free.
        There's more to find than bread and board:
        There's glory earned, and the dragon's hoard.
        In blood and ink the truth be poured.
    I break at your tears, but not at your plea."

II

1. At once Fin was gone in the morning bright,
   Seeking his fate in the wide world.
   > In a moment he was made poor.
   > No food nor coin followed through the door,
   > But hope invincible and manly lore
   Had the banner of his heart unfurled.

2. Fin first travelled the darkest streets,
   The fear-swept alleys where none may tread.
   > And though he witnessed foul acts,
   > The poorest of men made poorer through their pacts,
   > And felt no fear of their attacks,
   He passed in silence while good men bled.

3. He said to himself as he journeyed through,
   "What good is bravery to this place?
   > No more can these evil lords be slain
   > Than we can revoke the curse of Cain.
   > No deed nor government can mandate their gain
   Until the seed of virtue blooms its face."

4. Next Fin passed to the downtown
    Where the will of man nearly touched the sky.
        He saw some rich who would not work,
        Who sold their sons to devil and Turk,
        For wealth tore down both kitchen and kirk,
    Who on fate's wheel their conscience fly.

5. Fin again passing, his judgment spoke,
    "I cannot fight the vices of the rich
        Any more than the vices of the poor.
        How can I counsel those beyond my shores?
        What brave oath to these men might be sworn?
    Or who could I kill when ever-living is the lich?

6. Next Fin passed right out of the city
    And found the rural lands no less in sin.
        They made a pretext of the simple life,
        Avoiding all modern vice and strife,
        While an ancient grudge ever bloodied the knife,
    Preferring old heresy to innovation.

7. "What can I say of these," gasped Fin,
    "Who use custom to never examine themselves?
        They hide their vice under tradition's cloak;
        Their father's virtues they invoke,
        As their conscience stews and starts to smoke.
    To them brave deeds are as faeries and elves."

III

1. Despairing to find a world to save,
    Wearied Fin began walking back toward his home-
        His spirit levelled by these grey times,
        Its history that moves without nature's rhymes;
        Its virtue that critiques but never climbs.
    He'd forsake the life of action and turn to dust upon
        some tome.

2. A sudden cry startled his blood:
    The voice of a girl being beaten.
        Without a thought he ran toward her.
        There was no doubt that could deter,
        Or fear of danger to make unsure,
    Not of being bludgeoned or cooked and eaten.

3. He saw the girl being choked on the playground,
    Between the monkey bars and the slide,
        By a boy tremendous and ogre-like,
        Encircled by his gang upon muddied bikes,
        Waving their sticks as halberd and pike,
    As children and parents watched and cried.

4. "Suzanne! Suzanne!" Her mother called,
   "If you defend yourself, you're an aggressor.
       This boy is quite poor, it will be classist.
       And using male-like violence is inherently sexist.
       If he has mental health issues it could be ableist.
   I'll return with a solution; I must consult my professor."

5. But Fin cared not for these fantasies.
   He only cared to help the weak.
       He jumped and dashed through the guard line,
       His fists in the sunlight seemed to shine,
       For justice alone his heart did pine:
   One blow turned the bully into a swollen freak.

6. Parents wept in fear of nature's blood.
   Her mother cried again, "Suzanne,
       For being saved by a prince,
       Bound by the chains of romance,
       I sentence you to this penance:
   Attend public school and let experts your life plan."

7. Suzanne was promptly jailed from her liberator,
   And the bully made a teacher's assistant.
       Fin stood victorious and confused,
       Feeling defeated though fully unbruised
       But then in the gravel by his shoes:
   A lock of Suzanne's hair dark and resplendent.

IV

1. Who was watching from the bushes?
   It was not another child,
       Not another fussy grownup,
       Not a counselor to lock the boy up,
       Not wily beast nor playful pup,
   But a king, a lawful lord, firm and mild.

2. Fin stood confirmed in the life of action,
   And yet unclear of where to go,
       Feeling he left when he should have been sent.
       Then he saw the king pointing toward a tent.
       In enchanted silence they together went
   To the camp where the Eagle's banners flow.

3. "How can you be here in this land of equality?"
   The king smiled gently and answered Fin,
       "There's always a king when one is needed,
       Wherever the law is no longer heeded,
       And love is by liberty unseated.
    When democracy turns to vice, the brave will turn to
   him."

4. At this the king began a discourse
   On the history of nobility and their rights.
      "As all have in Adam a common sire,
      Not in blood does nobility have its first fire,
      But in bold deeds at times most dire
   Does the nobility of nature show its true lights.

5. "But as sons receive the ways of their fathers,
   And society needs acknowledge difference,
      The honour of blood is laid in law;
      Civic nobility deserves our awe.
      Though less pure than virtue raw,
   Deeds as well as goods form an inheritance."

6. Having finished his history,
   The king declared Fin would receive arms.
      In swearing to the crown his fealty
      He would receive honour in perpetuity.
      No longer an impulse, but now a duty,
   Would be his vow to save from harm.

7. Fin kept the vigil in the royal chapel.
   By prayer and fasting he was prepared.
      Then he received the cleansing bath,
      A white robe that purity guide his path,
      A red cloak to risk blood against tyrant's wrath,
    Stockings brown as the earth where in death he will be
       snared,

8. Gold spurs to swiftly follow the divine commandments,
   And lastly the sword with two edges sharp:
   > One justice, one loyalty, rightly wed,
   > That with the same blow by which the tyrant's bled
   > The peace is secured, and the peasant is fed,
   That War's music may sound orderly as song of harp.

9. Lastly the king gave him a blow,
   "Arise my knight, now Sir Phinees.
   > You must bring honour to this new name.
   > Be not content with pageantry of fame.
   > You've learned there's a king, now learn my shame:
   My land is oppressed by a dragon contrarious."

V

1. On Phinees' shield was the royal Eagle,
   Next to it the loyal Hound.
   > Between the two a Cross of gold,
   > That deeds done for fealty, however bold,
   > Would by a greater love be dolled
   Than what is due to any mortal prince crowned.

2. In his hand he held the lock of hair,
   By his side the deadly blade.
   > He saw before him charges two,
   > A dragon to kill for honor true,
   > And by the duty given when love strikes through,
   Suzanne to free in a jail raid.

3. In her room alone quietly she wept,
   Lamenting her material safety.
   > How could she be satisfied with a child's life,
   > Worrying about snack time, never to be a wife,
   > Competing in games without real strife,
   Encouraged in self-esteem without sanity?

4. "And how," Spoke Suzanne,
    "Can I share my mother's concerns
        When these mental shackles paralyze her,
        And happiness can't bloom inside her?
        The life of virtue she cannot deter.
    Does good stand still as the blind world churns? "

5. Suzanne stared with longing out her window,
    The stars seeming more real than her home,
        When she heard a knock upon the pane,
        Tiny pebbles began to rain,
        Her sorrow suddenly did wane:
    From the street Fin shone like a star in the dome.

6. In mail and in the helmet bright,
    The blazoned shield at his side,
        Seeing her he called, "It is I, your Fin,
        Sir Phinees now, your favor here to win.
        When I doubted my life, by despair did sin,
    Devotion to you secured my manly pride."

7. "I thank you, brave Sir," Suzanne replied,
    "And I've longed for you again to rescue.
        But my jailer is my mother and my queen.
        I'm held by piety in bonds unseen.
        I'll not run off like some barbarous teen.
    You will chain my true strength if you free my body."

8. "Then every third night I'll come to you,
   That you always may hope for a life uncaged."
       "Dear Phinees, I will be more free
       Devoted to you in captivity
       Than in disobedience I ever could be.
   In freedom interior is romance enlarged."

VI

1. Phinees went out in search of the dragon,
   But found no sign of its bloody wrath.
      Throughout the kingdom men spoke peace,
      And even the poor seemed to feast,
      Luxury poured down from the great to the least,
   Roads of commerce over-paved the warrior's path.

2. All seemed to say it was the best of times
   In which man had lifted himself above nature.
      No more to be pulled by blind evolution,
      But riding the waves of revolution
      In technology and institution,
   Humanity could now decide its future.

3. For a month and more Phinees thus wandered,
   Each third night sharing Suzanne's loneliness.
      Even the problems he once saw-
      Gangs and usurers with gaping maw-
      Seemed by the light of this age to thaw.
   Having now a duty, he could find no true distress.

4. Each time he enquired of one suffering
   He received a shocking response:
      "Look ye back to the times of torture
      When blind tribes prospered by murder,
      And life was nought but crushing labor.
   We live in the first dawn of innocence.

5. "For the nations have become humanity,
   And there's no one left to war against.
      We no longer suffer by invisible fate,
      But due to technical problems that soon will abate
      When we collect enough data, so quicken the rate!"
   Phinees saw they were by a demon entranced.

6. Strange, now that he served a lord
   That king was nowhere to be found.
      Ruler and dragon both were absent,
      And human motives were now thought indecent
      To explain the cruelty of master and subject.
   All law was measured right into the ground.

VII

1. For a year and then for many years
   Phinees saw the world improve.
       He tried to inspire Suzanne, his love,
       To keep her heart set on things above,
       And hope against nature for the coming dove,
   But with no great conquest she grew harder to move.

2. Fin began to wonder, "Am I mad,
   Believing I once swore loyalty to a king
       Who since then has remained unseen?
       By long travel I grow wild and lean,
       While perhaps I never did properly ween;
   Perhaps it's more natural to speak than to sing."

3. Every third night he still saw Suzanne,
   But he now grew more curious about her school.
       Had he failed her by never learning?
       Was he deceived by irrational yearning?
       But it was too late to begin turning
   His life toward useful work and office rule.

4. Still he found some pleasantness.
    His mother leapt, "my Fin returns!"
         Happy was she to receive him,
         To feed and clothe and educate him,
         And never wonder what's inside him,
    So long as a body's safe from bruises and burns.

5. Whether he held the ideal or only inertia,
    Every day after oatmeal he roamed the earth
         In search of any sign of adventure,
         That the world come of age his heart could nurture.
         Or must he be content with what all men sought for:
    Comfort and ease, friendship and mirth?

6. And yet the more his luxury grew,
    So grew his wild desperation.
         No more did virtue drive his errantry,
         Nor did he only go out habitually,
         But some animal force kept him unhappy.
    Depression became crooked inspiration.

7. Suzanne and his mother started to worry.
    Their fretting made him grow indignant.
         Their love could not guide him toward his goal,
         And as he could no longer see the whole
         Of virtue spilling from a heart made full,
    Mere care for his happiness appeared repugnant.

8. For the second time in his life he was saved by a cry.
   Blood called to blood, and Phinees did fly
      Across the obvious pleasures of the lawn,
      Across the electric city's frantic yawn,
      To where an old man was set upon
   By compassionate strangers commanding him to die.

VIII

1. "What good are you with all your preaching?
   You're a walking corpse ordained to be a fossil.
         We've solved the equation of human flourishing.
         Your bread is just word, we manufacture what's
            nourishing.
         That your life still lingers is more than discouraging.
   Current research suggests it is you we should kill."

2. So spoke the scrawny thugs to the black robed man.
   Phinees wasted no time in drawing his blade.
         They cursed and blasphemed as their heads rolled,
         Their blood's first warmth after a life of cold.
         A thousand blog updates their innocence told.
   The old man alone spoke, "Justice our age has now
      arrayed."

3. In thanks he offered hospitality.
   "I possess little, but I give you my all.
         I have no gold to pay you tribute,
         Nor trumpeters to play a grand salute,
         Only a meal of wild berry and root.
   Come receive my poverty and renew your call."

4. They travelled long on aching feet,
    Out of the city's grid of might,
        Past the slums ever improving,
        Past Fin's neighborhood ever middling,
        Past country estates ever decaying,
    Past wilderness to nowhere, past all sight.

5. In dark through desert guided by stars,
    Till the light of heaven faded to perfect black.
        Guided then by the age-worn dragging feet,
        Trusting he would approach to wisdom's seat,
        Though the night deprived him of all thought and
            heat.
    Suddenly in the sky dripped light from a stony crack.

6. Guided by this muted consolation,
    They climbed sheer cliffs they could not see.
        With no chirping of the midnight cricket,
        No hunting beast, no fox nor owlet,
        No night blossom or thorny thicket.
    Mixt with fear and hope climbed Phinees free.

7. The dim crack within the sky
    Now shone a world within a mountain.
        With one last pull Phinees arose
        And stared with wonder at golden rows
        Of reliefs lit by lamps ever aglow,
    From endless oil in a natural fountain.

8. The gold seemed part of the cavern itself.
   There all of history was given form:
      From the Spirit's first breath upon the water,
      Man's first home near the world's first river,
      The nomads expelled and forced to wander,
   All peoples incubated in a world-wide storm.

9. Then grew the Idol's kingdoms from the altar
   Where once our fathers had seen the truth.
      Spilling blood for this world's lord,
      The kings of earth gathered their hoards,
      Freemen were held by the slaver's cord.
   For the poor there was no ruth.

10.   Empire trampled empire,
     Till all gave way to Rome.
        The relief curved round the cavern wall,
        The lord's of earth on knees did fall,
        Offering tribute to the Lord of all,
     Looking down from a central dome.

11.   Below that dome an altar stood,
     The black robed man there incensing.
        He blessed the image of the God-bearer,
        Crushing dragon with feet warlike and fair,
        And Joseph who was the demons' terror,
     Lastly tabernacle with angels adoring.

12.   He turned then to incense Sir Phinees,
        Who bowed by instinct ancient and clear.
           The man spoke at last, "Bernardus am I,
           Who here unites the low with the high,
           Unites now sun and moon in a new sky:
        The last priest and last knight in holy fear."

IX

1. Courage lies not in constant daring.
   Justice is more than pity for the weak.
   >In a dark age the heroes grow dark.
   >On the path of beatitude none embark,
   >Nor discover new lands on the fisherman's barque.
   Soon heroes bring only sarcasm, and of loyalty none may
   speak.

2. Most of all it's peace we do not know.
   Not merely forgiveness instead of vengeance.
   >Not only the absence of bloody battles,
   >Or civil debates without saber rattles,
   >But even while being poisoned or bound in nettles:
   The perfect peace of a clean conscience.

3. Without this surpassing peace a hero cannot ascend.
   Phinees saw this truth in a single moment.
   >He confessed his sins whole and entire.
   >Contrition filled him with zealous fire,
   >While Fin was consumed on the interior pyre.
   Bathed in the bloodless bath he to the altar went.

X

1. Receiving the Word by hearing;
   Knowing the Word as fleshy loaf:
       Phinees saw the order of creation,
       From low to high all in their station,
       Seraphim and stone receiving right ration,
   All bound to all by ancestral oath.

2. He saw the laws that cannot be measured,
   Ideas being more real than numbers.
       Experiment dealing with parts in extention
       Of beings that require unextended formation
       For there to be a law that can govern their motion:
   Useless knowledge thus soars while technology slumbers.

3. There is a Law before all law,
   And a Being before all being;
       A Nature without nature;
       A diversity without fracture.
       While blind philosophers see a history of rupture,
   The mind unbound never ceases to sing.

4. Phinees saw there was an unillumined light,
   Dark and shining from above the sky,
       While forms living and intelligent
       Behind the air were ever sent
       To bear that light below the tent
   Where mutable man camps waiting to die.

5. He knew the Image of all Creation.
   While experts argue about the shape of mere galaxies,
       Small in size and with few dimensions,
       With certainty he knew the rational emanation
       By which all law is an election,
   Which alone reveals man's dark complexity.

6. He saw the world turned upside down:
   Not merely some problems to be corrected.
       In man's wisdom sense was called certainty,
       And the mind an accident of complexity,
       But Phinees saw this was absurdity:
   No true knowledge from particulars alone can be
       collected.

7. Likewise the world did not just fail in virtue.
   Men do not strive for the light and simply fall short,
       But they fill up their bodies and hate their own souls;
       They announce their achievements and fatten the
           bull;
       To actualize the future, self-worship's the toll.
   They make the world flat and close every port.

8. Those who are left behind are not the poor
   Who by the love of man daily grow fatter,
      But those who have the sight to see their failure,
      And are then diagnosed with despair,
      For malfunction of optimism put in medical snare.
   Yet the Good News received, our evil need not matter.

9. Having seen all worlds and works of man,
   He saw at last the dragon long sought:
      Burning within the belly of the earth,
      Ever swallowing and giving brith,
      Gnawing man's bones clean of all worth,
   Laboring engines of bloody will and iron wrought.

10.   Thousands of heads to gaze upon our every dwelling
      Bursting from the terrestrial crust.
         It seemed the true lord of this sphere,
         Bloating man with rights and good cheer,
         Boiling him with hope and fear:
      A nightmare god who governed man by ancient trust.

XI

1. Suzanne knew that something must change.
   Long had she indulged Fin's fantasy.
   > At times he seemed somewhat to recover,
   > But then he'd start his story over.
   > She wondered if he'd ever love her,
   If her life full-bloomed might outshine all childhood
   ecstasy.

2. And now he'd been gone for weeks.
   Was he on some new delusion?
   > Whatever his failings, he'd always been dutiful.
   > Their three day ritual to her remained beautiful,
   > Though of its origin she had long been doubtful.
   How she longed for his return, yet to be free of illusion.

3. She stared blankly at the night with aching memory,
   Recalling how once Fin shone like the stars.
   > But in youth everything seems magic.
   > Without responsibility, those feelings become tragic.
   > The seed's only good if you find how to crack it.
   Once the window was her freedom, now her jail bars.

4. Growing more sleepless as her eyes grew tired,
   The night seemed now strangely living,
        Like a hot breath that covered the city,
        A writhing skin that hugged the world snugly,
        A loving dark that saw her truly.
   She felt no surprise to see great eyes gazing.

5. Large lights of orange, serpentine and smart,
   With the calm rationality of a bonfire.
        Suzanne felt at last she was understood.
        Blood returned to her heart of wood.
        To be seen for herself, for her own good…
   Then she saw the teeth, and trembled inside her.

6. Suzanne stood frozen in thankful fear.
   To live or die now seemed the same,
        So long as she could be somewhere new,
        So long as this hot breath could melt the glue,
        And claws clear the vines that around her grew.
   She stared in the eyes and said, "Speak my name."

7. "Suzanne," shook a voice gentle with horror.
   "How long have you waited to be with us?
        The world's full grown and ready for you.
        The smoke is cleared that once separated you.
        Analysis will cleanse the myths that isolate you.
   If you will become like me, I will make Fin like us."

XII

1. "O Master! O Teacher! I am not strong.
   To fight man's wickedness I can do a little.
       But what of this Beast older than the dirt,
       Cast in fire before man's first hurt,
       Whose talons melt through plated shirt,
   And eyes rot the heart with wordless riddle?"

2. Bernardus, unmoved, sipped from a jar.
   "All the calculations of man are false,
       And every legend precise and true.
       An army may fall before one or two,
       As is written for the eyes of the few.
   Blowing horns may topple those scaly walls.

3. "It has long been sung that a knight prevails
   If he loves a lady and faithfully serves her,
       If he's loyal to his lord above his self,
       If he loves honour more than wealth,
       If trials and fasting are his health,
   So ride your charge with lance pointed and sure."

4. Now Phinees was vested as a true chevalier.
   The Eagle and Hound his banners adorned.
   > He rode a white horse fast as sunlight,
   > His lance like lightning, and twice as bright,
   > An icon of humility and magnanimous might,
   Toward a world of demons for charity scorned.

5. The hill once dark and impossible
   Now seemed to light the earth below.
   > In mountain gold was his armor detailed:
   > His shining countenance by the cavern scaled.
   > Across unmapped desert he now sailed:
   An image to reveal but not to show.

XIII

1. Men in seats of power much evil have invented,
   But often the decision of a woman unremarkable,
      Ever ignored by history,
      Not even noted as a mystery,
      By some small consent made domestically,
   Moves the age by power invisible.

2. So began a transformation.
   Where once men were divided in warring factions,
      The line between city and country was erased,
      Distinction of rich and poor was erased,
      Scale of smart and stupid was erased,
   As the peace of fire united all in action.

3. A caucophany of voices filled the earth.
   "Let us sign more contracts than ever before!"
      "Let us declare a festival for eating pie!"
      "Let us listen to Zeppelin and get super high!"
      "Let us hurt no creature till the day we die!"
   "Let us give everyone more and more!"

4. "Let us make a law that everyone plays guitar!"
   "Let us edit our brains to always be happy!"
       "Let us have no law but to always be cool!"
       "Let us declare that love is our only rule!"
       "Let us be free to love any man, any mule!"
   "Let us develop an app to help us dress snappy!"

5. "Let us make a book full of dumb facts!"
   "Let us write down and discuss our dreams!"
       "Let us make a car that's easy to drive!"
       "Let us gift the bees with a really nice hive!"
       "Let us to the depths of the ocean dive!"
   "Let us declare life is as good as it seems!"

6. Enlightened with this obvious clarity,
   Upright Man began to hunch.
       His back was bent and his skin turned green.
       Being ever so nice made him ever so mean,
       Ideal ever mixed with spleen.
   A goblin army was born over lunch.

7. Through the window Suzanne was lifted,
   And now rode on the dragon's head.
       Free at last from the waiting life,
       Free to rule as queen and wife,
       Free to find Fin and silence his strife:
   Commander of the goblin horde, the living and the dead.

XIV

1. Phinees could not give men what they deserved,
   For they had merited worse than death.
   > But he sliced through the butcher and the baker,
   > Lopped off the head of the candlestick maker,
   > Without distinction killed slave and banker,
   And all other frightful creatures worthy of wrath.

2. He killed the president and executed traitors.
   The working class lay dead in their own vomit.
   > In rage he ended the good work of activists.
   > He silenced the prayers of the humanists.
   > Set fire to the homes of libertarians and communists.
   On library and school he crashed like a comet.

3. Phinees slew thousands, but their numbers were endless.
   The orcish hordes grew always greater,
   > For the peace-loving age had secured every weapon.
   > They blasted with rifle and with cannon,
   > Then missiles and bombs and chemical weapon.
   To preserve their traditions they'd spare no torture.

4. They sent out a doctor to tell him he's ill;
    They sent a historian to teach about progress;
        A meditation instructor to remind him to breath.
        They gifted him with strips to whiten his teeth,
        And found him a tutor to help him to read,
    While bomb and bullet corrected his excess.

5. Neither storm of fire nor wind of doctrine
    Could knock Phinees from his horse.
        He saw he never enough could kill
        To make at last the world hold still,
        Though greatly was he improved by the thrill.
    At last for the dragon he set his course.

XV

1. Suzanne made the world fat by her justice,
   And made the mind a lump once more.
   > What was begun in the age of man–
   > Universal compassion in the service of man–
   > Was now complete in the end of man,
   Made perfect in the beast's dumb roar.

2. Man when in honour did not understand,
   He was compared to a beast and made like unto them.
   > Suzanne gave discourse on the flat earth,
   > Our world stretched forever without any girth,
   > Endless motion and change without any birth,
   A world with no depth or edges to hem.

3. *O silent earth, anticipating prophecy!*
   "What is truth?" Spoke she, "and what is virtue?
   > Every being is tiny balls of something crashing,
   > Or if not that then it's strings vibrating,
   > Or else mathematical laws emanating.
   How can one and not another bit of moving stuff be
   true?

4. "No truth without mind, and there is no mind.
   No thought without the animal part,.
       No animal without the chemical substance,
       No molecules without atomic elements,
       Down and down until the smallest instance.
   O deny your existence and lift up your hearts.

5. "No truth without mind and there is no mind.
   Nothing we know can be what it is.
       If you know it's composite, then you see clearly.
       What does it matter the final theory?
       Whether it's atoms or lightning we may change our
           mind yearly.
   If there is no true whole then there's nothing that is.

6. "We call this bit of brain 'I think the earth is round,'
   And call this bit, 'I know it's flat.'
       But stuff moving through space cannot be true or
           false.
       The judgments of thought cannot be true or false
       Any more than one rock is true and another is false.
   Free from judgment we see the universe flat.

7. "No truth without mind, and there is no mind.
   I'm a unicorn as much as I am an ocean.
       Every idea is as true as iron or coal.
       An idea is material parts and nothing is whole,
       Atheism and religion just bits in your skull.
   So live every way and live every notion."

XVI

1. Sir Phinees to the dark tower came,
   Searching there for Elfland's queen.
   > Beyond the fields of goblin dead
   > Steel buildings twisted in formless dread,
   > An unalive creature without mind or head
   Grew ever fat and blackened ever lean.

2. Through metal he cut easily as flesh.
   Nor was he disturbed by the earth quaking
   > As tentacle girders consumed the city
   > His mind remained bright, gentle, and witty.
   > Till he came to the door shut more than tightly,
   Impenetrable by fist and by sword raking.

3. "Open," spoke he, but the door only laughed.
   "Open," spoke he, and two faeries arose
   > In girlond greene and hair like sunne,
   > Thinking with man to have their fun.
   > "Take fruit of Arcady, eat nutty bun,
   Easilie the door you'll open and close.

4. "Eat like us and see our Eden,
   Eyes open, see unity of pavement and soil.
       In the beginning Gaia gave her fruits freely
       To show God and nature loved man dearly.
       In tower dark, earth gives again treely.
   Eat of fae food, leave your punishing toil."

5. "Ne'er can I leave manhood to 'scape my meted doom.
   O froward fae, fie on your false innocence!
       Fie on your words so falsely mild.
       You give back not my nature, but the guilt of a child.
       You grow not a garden but wend the world wild.
   Your food is not seasoned with reasonable resonance."

6. "Spice the cake and eat, if only you'll eat.
   What tricks have we to trick the law?
       Without eyes of flesh you see nothing of space.
       Seraphim exalted cannot look in your face.
       Can you see our kingdom if you dine not with our
           race?
   To enlighten your eyes, only unhinge your jaw."

7. "Then let me eat as one who contributes to the feast."
   Taking holy water, Phinees washed the fruit.
       Taking blessed salt, he sprinkled the cake.
       Spoke, "All honour to God who for our sake
       Did divers worlds and divers creatures make."
   He broke the bread as elfs offered praise of flute.

8. Consuming their verdict, they changed, one better one
   worse.
   One greater in size, flowering, regal,
       Grew red in tooth and green in nail.
       His face bloated like a landed whale.
       In judgment robes he spoke, "Sir Knight, to jail!
   I've examined your doings; they are most illegal."

9. The smaller then hardened and cracked like shell of
   beetle.
   Out came a bird of rainbow feather,
       With the face of a woman cut in stone, yet tender.
       She answered the judge, "tell me who is the lender
       Who calls to account our chivalrous pretender?"
   "It's the lady who walks on scales soft as heather."

10. "But he was born before her reign,
    And received arms from another."
        Then grinned the most wise and pus-filled judge,
        "But he has brought our queen a grudge.
        As she raised herself from the mind's dark sludge,
    Now he comes to slay that beastly mother.

11. "As she has tamed the monstrous spirit of the world,
    So all born of the world owe her subjection."
        Replied the bird, "O liberty of devouring,
        From our Queen and Mother at all times
            showering,
        That we spiritual worms no more hide cowering,
    To the knight who devours our law can there be
        objection?"

12.   *O Bird of Paradise! O Muse of Stone!*
      Her justice surpassed all argument.
            For at that word she showed her cruel teeth,
            Leapt on the judge, crying, "obedient thief!"
            She ate first his liver, then pulled spine from its
                  sheath.
      Phinees, right fed, entered easily the royal tenement

XVII

1. As earth is larger than all space,
   As history is longer than all time,
       As tears of the Immaculate surpass all weeping,
       As martyr's hour proves our love unfeeling,
       And heavenly vault shows our rust unkeeping,
   So did the joy of man prove elfkin without rhyme.

2. Here where reason's law the world unnatured,
   In tower dark coiled over the flattened globe,
       Goblin men at last walked with spirit.
       No angelic ladder, no need to fear it:
       A world of one dimension, matter cherubic...
   While one stood upright, the sky would now disrobe.

3. His armor was the sun, his shield the moon,
   His sword the lightning bolt of wisdom.
       He rode his charger named Free Choice of Will,
       With two spurs called Temperance and Keeping Still.
       His helmet was Courage Blind to Thrill.
     He shone with judgment, without blow rending enemy
       dumb.

4. Though easily he could fall many thousand more,
   All were speechless as light entered the tower:
       In seeing a man lawful and free
       Each saw what he was and could not be,
       Many sunk to the ground, few raised to the knee
   As unreasonable light shook forth reasons power.

5. All lukewarm souls caked and crumbled as a mouth of
       dust.
   Passionate goblins became true beasts.
       Faery found a more diverse fate:
       Some into wind and fire and all force great,
       Some manticore, and werewolf, and fell things of
           hate,
   One alone in all creation joined the angelic feast.

6. The world was then enchanted,
   Though the dragon's work undone.
       Wherever there is manly love
       There is clarity 'tween monster and dove,
       Burning hell below, heaven's flame above.
   Arms and not letters sure Vision has won.

XVIII

1. Not in vision from a mountaintop
   Not as serpent force wrapt through all dirt,
      But black of scale, eyes cold with fire,
      A living fortress with mind that cannot tire.
      Phinees wept with pity as his eyes moved higher:
   There the enchantress reigned inert.

2. Though none by might could stand against him,
   Nor bow his head by syllogism,
      Love that holds the heavens aloft may dim the sense
         of man;
      Love that guides to virtue may depend on a woman;
      Love that subdues great armies may be smitten by
         her ban,
    And the love that colors all the world may be shoved
      back in the prism.

3. She was turned black but beautiful,
   Terrible as an army set in array.
      "O enchantress," spoke he, "Pour your name out as
         oil
      Upon my dry lips, worn chapped with toil,
      Corrupted through lack of praise for one so royal.
    O hair as a flock of tigers, breasts as snow in May!"

4. These words the witch was quick to answer.
   "My low-lovely slave who shakes every nerve,
       Is murder and vengeance now your game?
       Is your mind turned foolish for lack of my name?
       Strength is your weakness, pride is your shame.
   If you can, come and kill the one you serve."

5. "Though this vision now knots my mind," spoke the
       knight,
   "No woman's blood do I wish to spill.
       Not as a slave, but as one by love moved
       Freely to thy service, even now I'm soothed
       To save you from the dragon bile-toothed.
   Sincerely I attempt praise and seek thy liberty still."

6. "If you insist you must kill me, you won't find it easy.
   The Queen of all Life deals death very swiftly.
       If you are my servant then it's my right to kill,
       No self-defense needed, only the thrill
       Of driving my teeth, rending flesh at will.
   I gnaw with chaos and disorganize deftly."

7. With speed greater than shield, strength over sword,
   In one straight bolt pierced talon through breast.
       Where is the mother to weep for the son?
       Where is the bard wailing lamentation?
       Where is nature to rise against what is done?
   Flood canyons with your tears, make death your heart's
       guest.

XIX

1. "My Daemon, my body, my all-living genius!
   You promised to bring my true love to me,
      To kill courtly illusion and save me the man,
      But without consultation you've changed the plan.
      You've removed the heart with our truth bearing
         talon.
   What good a world to rule if man dies with his fantasy?"

2. "Not dead," hummed a hiss, "but emptied out.
   Soon you will see that the mind is my clay.
      From my tongue I will drip seven drops of poison
      Daily at dusk 'til the week's conclusion
      Sees his mind made ready for your love potion.
   Watch with pleasure and longing for that eighth day!"

3. The first dose made our hero a prophet,
   Ever vomiting newspapers into the sky.
      Rejoice all ye peoples for current opinion!
      Weep at every drama as if cutting an onion!
      The witch clapped at the reform of her dungeon,
   To see her love's distraction turned toward matters high.

4. A second drop of poison showed him shapely and nude.
   Lament that one so athletic ever was covered in armor,
      Muscular symmetry hidden in symbols of virtue,
      That soul had overshadowed a power so true.
      Her contempt waning, she admired the view.
   O unclothed simplicity! O original ardor!

5. Three deadly drops made him praise the world's order,
   How nature moved all by its occult power.
      The great pulse of Life shone through the dead stars,
      The bubbling ooze coursed through angels and cars:
      No law outside itself, no cold jail bars.
   The strength of that dead motion drove him from that
      hour.

6. O life giving poison! In only four drops
   One unbraved could praise the apotheosis of machines.
      What never could be done by the flame of life
      Was easily accomplished by automatic knife,
      Eternally cutting, efficient without strife.
   O witch, see nature's power perfected without being.

7. With five drops the work seemed almost done.
   Thinking by living, the bare-chested prophet
      Said, "Calm down, O World, do not get excited.
      By holding convictions, passion is ignited.
      Wars are begun when we perceive wrongs to be
         righted."
    O Queen, here's your man of peace with white linen
      gauntlet.

8. All praise to drop six, the dream of equality!
   Without dogma of war, what argument for headship?
       O brown haired no one, crowned first by his
           madness,
       Then clothed in black robes, coronated in sadness,
       Sane again, he sees the girl, merely nice, bringing
           gladness.
   Does it please you, great witch, this sensible friendship?

9. The seventh drop erased all others.
   No need for opinion when all minds are equal.
       No ground for scientific progress
       When hope for honour is always excess.
       No need to tolerate what never can digress.
   Praise autonomous agreement, new ground of the civil.

10.   O heart of the world, Queen of earth's light,
       Hear your beloved speak of consent and contract!
           Removing ideas, you've unfreed his will,
           Liberated your liberator with gentle skill,
           Protected your soft hands from his tendency to
               kill.
       How purely the free consent of atoms living beings
           may attract.

XX

1. Clothed in white by blackest hands,
   In delicate lace by gentle scale,
   > The Queen prepared for her wedding day.
   > What remained of her subjects staged a play:
   > Unenlightened, unslain, a dance vicious and gay.
   They surrounded the serpent, sang "Empress, Hail."

2. One imitated ooze then danced like algae
   As others stamped like flame and swirled like ocean,
   > Till algae crawled into hungry wolf,
   > Then lusted free with satyrs hoof.
   > Imagining stars on that steel roof,
   Violent contemplation wiggled out a man-like motion.

3. How that Man leapt with joy to carry his head!
   A mind-tooled animal, upright out and in.
   > He commanded the fire that bubbled around him,
   > The dance moved orderly around the beast's rim,
   > Singing, "force of survival, it's time that you skim
   This cumbersome tool out of our skin."

4. In the midst of their dancing the dragon sunk low,
   Pressing its hindparts into the mud.
      "Behold," growled the music, "how I copulate
      To bring a new race to this spinning blue plate.
      In this marriage at last man's survival is sate,
   His ways are sloughed off, he brings forth a bud.

5. "O bone and sinew, as styrofoam rise.
   Mind untrapped by curdled gray sponge,
      Body unbirthed by disfiguring blood,
      Nail that mind to a silicon stud,
      Magic's laws turn bile into soapy sud,
   Clean from cancer, from the mess of Self we lunge."

6. The lady reigning then began her speech:
   "In this violence at last is the ease I longed for.
      I think on my youth and see my dreams fulfilled.
      As a child it seemed easy, that none would be killed.
      United without struggle, I must now be thrilled.
   Do I contain nothing else, having emptied my store?"

7. She looked on her love and saw she despised him.
   His strength had become ornamental;
      His endless youth reduced to good looks;
      His searching genius now content with books;
      His devotion to her, crude emotional hooks;
   His vision of longing now sentimental.

8. "My Phinees," spoke she, "before we drink
   This draught of union without blame,
        As you no more may challenge me
        With imaginations no one can see,
        Nor force the marital idolatry,
   Speak one last time my name."

9. "Susannah," he echoed,
   "By the elders you stand accused.
        Did you meet a strange youth in a private garden?
        For the lusts of this beast do you require pardon?
        Or were you drawn by the odor of honey and
            cinnamon,
   And are now by lechers abused?"

10.   Hearing the word, she tearfully sang,
       "Why buds desire, and what is truth?
            In a land of law my case might be argued.
            This place is unnatural and must be subdued.
            In praise I see your glory renewed,
       And I will not wonder if violence is the honour of
           youth.

11.   "O Muse at last I invoke thee,
       Who by troubadour knight has given me praise.
            Why in my subjects do I inspire dull lust,
            Or friendship, or silliness, or effeminate trust?
            I lifted myself as I was told I must,
       But those who submit to Lowness as Song will rise."

12. The dancing anarchs stopped for lack of leadership.
In her joy she imagined a king giving fiefdoms,
 An island for the squire to win,
 A chalice in the mount of Aaron's kin,
 A primal will to gather in
Slave and master as one filial kingdom.

13. One woman who sees right makes all end well.
Where beast loved earth our knight's sword was
 thrust.
 Through the deadly womb all death was pinned.
 Without argument he made error rescind
 The mindlessness in which virtue sinned,
And the joints of the land were freed from their rust.

14. "May it always be so," Susannah sang,
"May violence be youth's flowering glory,
 May love be youth's honor fair.
 Even if we do all else poorly,
 Let us marry before we grow too young.
Domestic life shining like martial story,
 Let us marry and suffer every mortal care.
May our lawless good give law its glory,
 And our elder youth be praised by every tongue."

ABOUT THE AUTHOR

Eric Lynndon Brooks is a working-class father of five living very close to the center of the world in Chicago, IL. In addition to being a master of his own destiny fighting to restore a lost civilization, he is also extremely boring. He rarely leaves his home other than to go to work or attend Mass, has few close friends, rarely eats at restaurants, hears live music, or travels for pleasure. He is, however, adored by his children who believe it is normal for men to wander the house reading poetry aloud.

To taunt, harass, praise, or exalt Eric, or to commission a poem, contact him at regressivepoet@gmail.com.

Printed in Great Britain
by Amazon

56673529R00040